The Red Marble:
A Story of Christmas

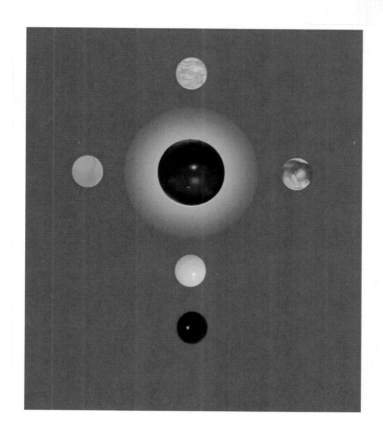

Written and Illustrated by
Kevin D. Finson

ISBN 9798582059967

Imprint: Independently Published

DEDICATION

This book is dedicated to my grandson, Leo. Leo loves the color red, and he also loves things that are shiny and bright. I hope this story will shine always in his heart, and he will live the kind of life Leo in the story strives to attain.

Give, and it will be given to you. Good measure, pressed down, shaken together, running over, will be put into your lap. For with the measure you use it will be measured back to you. (Luke 6:38)

THE RED MARBLE: A STORY OF CHRISTMAS

Leo awakened snuggled deep under the quilts and covers on his bed. The air in the house was chilly and smelled lightly of wood smoke. Leo could tell his daddy had just started the fire downstairs to warm the house. He imagined his mommy would be in the kitchen starting to make breakfast for everyone. She always made a traditional German breakfast on that day so everyone would be full and ready for the day. On the bedroom window was a pattern of frost that looked like delicate white and clear ferns from a magical forest. It felt good to snuggle under the covers in bed, but Leo knew this was an important day. This was the first day of the week before Christmas. Every year on that day, his family would go into town and shop for Christmas gifts. It was a good day to be with family because they would sing and drink hot chocolate and laugh with each other.

However, this year was going to be a little different. In years past, Leo could always figure out what to get for his daddy, his mommy, and his sisters. But this year Leo had one more gift to find. It had to be special, but he wasn't quite sure in what way it could be special. It was for a friend he had made at school. His friend was shy around most other kids. He often kept to himself, especially a recess and during lunch. In fact, Leo could not remember seeing his friend eat lunch. He never seemed to have brought anything with him to school to eat.

His friend's shoes were scuffed and worn, and his pants were clean but had some holes in the knees. His shirts were mended with patches of cloth that did not match the color of his shirts. Leo was not quite sure how he had first started talking to his friend, but they seemed to have formed a strong bond of friendship. Leo learned his friend's family was very poor, and Christmastime was particularly hard for them because they could not afford to buy gifts or special holiday food. They would not have candy canes, or sugar cookies, or simple toys. Leo asked his friend if he ever dreamed of getting certain toys, like a ball or bat, or like a small boat or something. His friend told Leo he had once seen some beautiful glass marbles he hoped some day he could get, but it was not likely it would ever happen. If he had some marbles he could put them in his pocket and have them with him all the time. But he and his family had come to expect very plain living without any such things. So Leo decided he would make his friend's Christmas special this year by giving him a gift. Leo had saved a few dollars through the year he got from small jobs like picking up sticks in yards, raking leaves, or walking neighbors' dogs. He planned to use that money to buy that special gift for his friend.

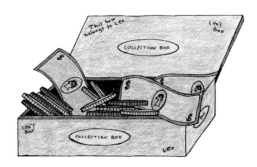

Leo's family babbled and giggled all through breakfast, and before long were putting on their coats to begin their journey into town. It was cold in the car, and everyone could see their breath as they crowded into their seats. The moisture from their breathing started to cloud up the inside of the car windows. Leo could feel the cold nipping at the tip of his nose and put his mitten up to his mouth to direct some warm air toward his nose to keep it thawed out. His daddy parked their car on Geschenk Street in front of a store in town and had everyone get out. He told them they could go up and down the street and shop in the different stores, but had to be back at the car in two hours. Then, Leo's daddy and mommy started walking one way, and Leo and his sisters walked another way, their feet crunching on the cold snow. He and his sisters stopped first at the shop where they could get some hot chocolate with a big marshmallow on top of it. The hot chocolate tickled their tongues and warmed them up beginning in their tummies. Soon they were ready to set out doing their gift shopping.

Leo's sisters left the store and started to walk along the sidewalk to another store to the south on Geschenk Street. But Leo did not go with them. For some reason he turned to walk north. His sisters were chattering amongst themselves and did not notice he was no longer with them. It was not long before Leo's sisters were out of sight and Leo found himself on an unfamiliar part of the street. He walked slowly, noticing the shops and buildings along the way. They were much older than the ones further south on Geschenk Street. It was obvious the owners of many of them had tried to keep them up, but just could not stave off the old age that wears down bricks and wood.

Soon, Leo came to a side street near the north end of Geschenk Street. It was Regalo Street. There was a pole at the north end of Geschenk Street showing where Regalo Street was located. Perhaps the pole once had the names of streets on it to direct people, but if it had those signs were now long gone. All that remained was the pole. Leo found himself turning down the side street to see what was there. It was then when he found the old toyshop.

Leo stood outside the toyshop looking through its front window. It was difficult seeing clearly through the window because of a layer of frost that was coating the glass. After trying to peer through the frosted glass a while, Leo decided it was time to go in. He reached and squeezed his fingers around the doorknob. It was an old iron doorknob with some kind of intricate design around its outer edge. In its center was some raised emblem that had been worn down to where it was barely legible. Leo slowly turned the doorknob and slowly pushed open the door. It creaked as it swung open, but it opened easily. Then Leo stepped into the toyshop and closed the door behind him.

Unlike the stores further south on Geschenk Street, this one was not well lit. There were some old pendulum-type lights hanging from the ceiling that gave out a warm but rather dull yellowish glow. It was enough to see things in the shop. The ceiling was one of those old tin-type ceilings where each of the square panels had some kind of raised design on it. They looked white,

but the light gave them a somewhat dingy appearance. Off to the left was a counter. It was very old and the wood in it showed cracks and dents. The counter showed several different layers of paint that had covered it over the years. Behind the counter and around the walls were wooden shelves that reached from floor to ceiling. Leo could tell great care had been taken in building those shelves because the front trim on them was carefully carved to show relief patterns of children and toys and vines.

Leo took a step forward and heard the floor creak beneath him. He looked down and saw a roughly-hewn wooden floor that was well-worn from the feet of many past visitors. There were knots in some of the floor planks, and there were places where the edge of one plank did not exactly fit flat against the next one. As he took a few more steps, Leo looked up again at the shelves. They were filled with all kinds of toys. They looked odd to him. There were small toys and large toys, and even in-between sized toys. There were carved wooden balls, boats, tops, dolls, chests, and so many other kinds of toys it was difficult to take them all in. The toys looked like they were very old, but when Leo looked closely at them they seemed to have a newness to them. They looked like they should have a thin covering of antique-shop dust on them, but each was spotlessly clean.

Suddenly Leo heard a voice. It was a gentle and deep man's voice with a warmth to its tone. Leo turned from the toy shelf to see a man standing behind the counter looking at him with quizzical eyes. "Can I help you with something?" the man asked. Leo stammered a bit and then said he was just looking around. Leo noticed none of the toys had price tags on them, so he asked the man how much the toys cost. The man smiled and said, "I don't really . . . sell . . . toys here."

Leo was puzzled, but turned back to look more at the shelved toys. The man said, "That's just fine. Look all you want. And Leo, if you find anything you like, just let me know." Leo was shocked. How did this man know his name? He had never met or even seen the man before, although he had a familiar look to him. Leo couldn't quite put his finger on why the man seemed familiar. "How do you know my name?" Leo asked. The man smiled but didn't say anything. He just smiled at Leo and said, "Take your time."

Leo stood there staring at the old man. His hair was white and long – slightly covering his ears. He had a white beard that had some curls to it. The man's eyes twinkled as if he knew Leo's most important inner secrets. Leo asked, "What is your name?" The man smiled and said, "Nick. Just call me Nick. That's what my friends call me." Leo

nodded his head slightly and shifted his eyes to the shelves behind Nick. The toys there were smaller than those on most of the other shelves in the shop. But the shelf that caught Leo's attention most was just behind Nick and above his head. Along the front edge of the shelf was a line of marbles. Each had been carefully placed in a holder so it could be easily seen. It was obvious to Leo that those were very old antique marbles. You just did not find those kind of marbles in stores today.

"Your marbles are pretty!" Leo said. Nick tilted his head back and slid his glasses down toward the tip of his nose and looked up at the shelf. "Yep, they are very special marbles. They are my most favorite things in my whole shop" Nick said. He asked Leo if he'd like to see them better. Leo grinned and nodded his head up and down. Nick reached up and pinched the first marble between his thumb and forefinger and slowly lowered it to the top of the counter. Leo crowded up against the front of the counter as close as he could so he could get a better look. He could feel the front edge of the wood pressing against his chest.

The first marble Nick held was white. He gently put it on the countertop in front of Leo. The shop light seemed to make the whiteness of the marble much brighter than it should have been. The marble was the purest white Leo had ever seen. As much as Leo looked, he could see no flaws in it. It was so white it seemed to glow from within. Leo asked, "Where did you get this marble from?" Nick smiled and said, "I was given that marble by two dear friends many years ago. They knew I liked marbles, so they gave me this one." Leo was intrigued. "Can you tell me about your friend?" he asked. Nick said, "There was a couple I knew. The man was about middle-aged and his wife was much younger. They didn't have much money and they were far from home. The wife was going to have a baby soon, and I saw them looking around for a place to spend the night, and I told them I would see what I could do to help them. All I could find was an old place next to an inn in a village. I was sorry I couldn't do better, but it was the best I could do. That night it came time for her to give birth to their child. He was a beautiful child and the stars shined brightly on him that night. A few days later they gave me this white marble to remember them by." Leo was silent as he absorbed the story.

"Want to see another one?" Nick asked. Leo said, "Sure!" So Nick tilted his head back and looked through his eyeglasses at the end of his nose and reached up and gently plucked another marble off the shelf.

This marble was a green one. It had swirling patterns of dark forest green moving through lighter holly and grass greens. Leo had never before seen such a marble. "Where did this one come from?" Leo asked. Nick smiled and said, "I was given that marble by some dear friends many years ago. They knew I liked marbles, so they gave me this one." Leo asked Nick if he would tell him about his friends.

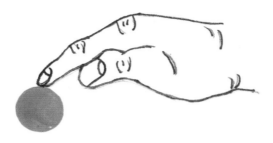

Nick smiled and began to share the green marble's story. "There were some folks who left their homeland seeking a better life for themselves. They got onto some sailing ships – you know, the old kind like the Pilgrims used. They spent many weeks sailing across the ocean. They were battered by storms and waves. Many thought they might end up lost at sea. One day they spotted a shoreline and sailed to it. The shoreline was covered with large rocks and boulders. It was not very hospitable, and not the kind of place to settle and build a village. But they were low on food and fresh water and had little choice but to start there. I came across them as they struggled to gather enough food to get them through the winter. They asked me if I could help them, and I told them I would see what I could do. Just a few days later I helped them find a nice meadow surrounded by lush forest. There was plenty of flat ground for them to plant their crops and plenty of game in the forest for them to hunt. They told me finding a place like that to live was a lifesaver for them. It wasn't long before they had their village built and were living a good life. They were able to raise enough food to send it to other new towns where people were struggling to thrive. When I was passing that way again I stopped to see them. I think it was just about this same time of the year. It was then when they gave me this green marble to remember them by." Leo sat silently, staring at the green marble, as he absorbed the story.

"Want to see another one?" Nick asked. Leo quickly said, "Yes" and anxiously awaited the next marble as he pushed himself closer against the counter. The wood creaked as Leo pressed his body against the counter. Nick tilted his head back and looked through his eyeglasses at the end of his nose and reached up and gently plucked another marble off the shelf.

This marble was a yellow one. Weaving back and forth between patches of yellow were golden streaks. They reminded Leo of ripe wheat just before harvest. "And what about this one?" Leo asked. Nick smiled and said, "A dear friend gave that marble to me many years ago. He knew I liked marbles, so he gave this one to me." Then Leo asked if there was a story about this marble, too. Nick smiled and said, "Yes, there is." Leo widened his eyes and raised his eyebrows as if asking Nick to share that story.

So Nick began. "I once knew a family who had packed everything they owned into a wagon and set off to find a new life out on the Great Plains. Their journey was long and often rough. At times they began to despair that they would find what they were seeking. But they kept going and one day came across some land that seemed perfect for them. The prairie spread out as far as the eye could see, and gently rolled up and down low hills. There was a small brook nearby. But as soon as they stopped and started to make their homestead, the weather turned very bad. Winds rushed in and battered their wagon and cabin. The sky grew dark and the thunder was loud and angry and rolled on for days. Lightning seemed to strike everywhere and the rain poured down so hard it began to wash away the sides of hills. Soon the rain became sleet and then blowing snow that blinded everything. The family was very fearful and huddled together in their small rough cabin to shelter from the storm.

I happened to be passing by and stopped in to see them. They told me how desperate they were and how frightened they were, and asked if there was anything I could do to help them. I told them I would see what I could do. The next morning I left their cabin and went on my way. Later that day the storm stopped and the sun came out. The sun glowed brightly that day and its warmth dried up the soil and started the prairie grasses to turn green. I came across that family again later that year – I think it was about this time of the year -- and they told me how the weather had been so good and they were able to grow their wheat and live a good life. Their wheat fields extend to the horizon and when the wind blew through them it was like waves on a golden ocean. Their wheat now is used to feed thousands of people. Then they gave me this marble to remember them by."

The toyshop seemed to be extra quiet now. Leo could hear himself breathing. "Want to see another one?" Nick asked. Leo nodded his head "Yes" and leaned over the countertop anxiously waiting to see the next marble. His elbows were now pressing down onto the old wooden countertop. So Nick tilted his head back and looked through his eyeglasses at the end of his nose and reached up and gently plucked another marble off the shelf. This marble was a blue one.

It was the deepest blue Leo had ever seen. It was like the deepest blue of the ocean mixed together with the bright blue of a clear spring sky. Leo asked, "What is this marble's story?" Nick leaned down and rested his elbows on the countertop not far from Leo's, gently touching the blue marble with the tip of his finger. "Well," Nick began, "this marble was given to me by a dear friend who knew I liked marbles. So he gave it to me." And Leo asked, "So . . . ?" And Nick shared another story.

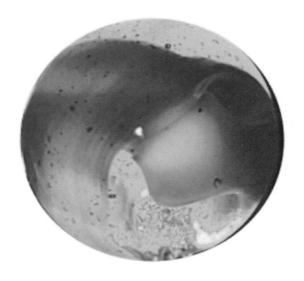

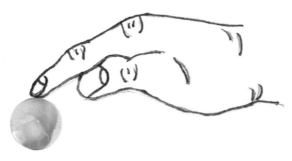

"I once knew a man who earned his living by fishing. He often fished alone. He had a small boat that he would take out onto a huge lake early each morning hoping to return to shore that evening with enough fish to sell. He set out one bright morning when the sky was blue and white fluffy clouds drifted lazily past him. The sun glistened off the low waves on the water. Unfortunately, he did not catch many fish that day. I happened to come across him that evening while he was rolling up his fishing nets and cleaning his boat. He told me about his day, and that he and his family would be hungry that night. He asked me if there was anything I could do to help. I told him I would see what I could do. The next day the man set out once again in his boat, and before noon his boat was full of fish. It seemed that each day after that the man could fill his boat with fish before the end of the day. I think it was a few weeks later when I came across the man by his boat early one morning. I think it was about this same time of the year. He told me about his fishing and how he harvested so many fish that he could share them with many people so they could have enough food to eat. Then he gave me this marble to remember him by." Leo sighed deeply. He had gone fishing with his daddy once in a while and returned home empty-handed. Luckily for them, his family did not have to rely on their fishing to feed themselves.

Then Nick asked, "Want to see another one?" Leo said, "Of course I would!" as he shifted his elbows on the countertop and rested his chin in his hands. So Nick tilted his head back and looked through his eyeglasses at the end of his nose and reached up and gently plucked another marble off the shelf.

This marble was a black one. It was the blackest of black, and it reminded Leo of the black of anthracite coal. He told Nick how it reminded him of coal, and Nick said, "What a coincidence! That is exactly part of the story about this marble!" Leo said, "Tell me, please tell me!"

So Nick began. "I had some dear friends in a small town who knew I liked marbles, so they gave it to me." Leo asked where the town was. Nick said it was a tiny town high up in the eastern mountains. The people who lived there were miners. They mined coal. It was a very hard and dangerous life. They were able to get just enough coal out of the ground to survive up in those mountains. One year, the company that bought their coal went out of business. So the townsfolk had no income to buy food and clothing. I happened to be passing through the mountains at that time and stopped to see the people there. They told me what had happened, and asked me if I could help. I said I would see what I could do. The next day a man showed up in the town asking to buy their coal. He was from a big coal company and they wanted the coal the townsfolk had been mining. Winter was coming, so this came just in time for everyone so they could make it through the harsh times. And they were able to mine enough coal to share it with other towns so they could get through harsh winters, too. About this same time of the year when I next came through that town the people told me what had happened, and they gave me this marble to remember them by."

Leo was starting to become tired, but he wanted to see one more marble. And there was just one more marble on the shelf. Nick noticed Leo's tiredness and asked, "There's one more left. Do you want to see it?" Leo said he did, and Nick said, "This is the most special of all the marbles I have. It is more precious to me than any of the others."

Leo's interest was piqued. "Why is it more precious than the others?" Nick said, "Because of how it came to be. It came to be because of a dear friend of mine. He knew I liked marbles, so he made this one and gave it to me." So Nick tilted his head back and looked through his eyeglasses at the end of his nose and reached up and gently plucked another marble off the shelf.

This marble was a red one. In fact, it was more than red. It was crimson. It was the deepest crimson Leo had ever seen – or even dreamed about.

20

Nick held it right in front of Leo's eyes and then slowly lowered it toward the countertop. But he did not put it on the counter. Instead, he held it carefully in the palm of his open hand.

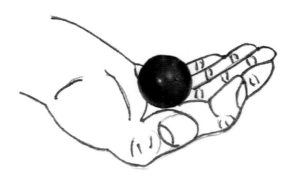

He let Leo reach out with his finger and slowly roll the crimson marble from side to side, over and back, frontwards and backwards. There were no swirls or marks in the marble. It was perfect. Except for a tiny white mark that seemed to be just beneath the surface of the marble. Leo squinted his eyes and peered at the mark. It almost looked like it was a snowflake. A pure white snowflake. Nick could tell Leo was excited to hear about this marble, so he began the story. "My friend was a teacher. He travelled all across the land teaching people about loving each other and how to live a good life. Many people would walk long distances to learn from him. My friend came to love those people. He loved them so much that he was willing to give them everything he had. In fact, he gave them his life. Not long after that I saw him again. If I recall it was just about this same time of the year. He gave me this marble to remember him by." I always carry this marble with me wherever I go when I travel so I keep him close to me."

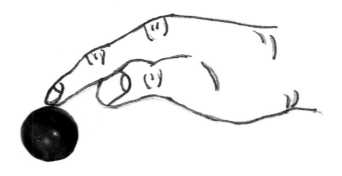

Leo pondered what Nick had shared with him about each of the marbles, but especially about the crimson red one. Leo said, "You sure have had some special friends!" Nick gently nodded his head up and down. "Yes, I have." Leo said, "I have been looking for a Christmas gift for someone special to me. I don't suppose I could buy one of these from you?" Nick smiled and said, "I really don't . . . sell . . . these toys." Leo sighed. Then Nick continued, "But you will get that special gift you are searching for." Tears started to well up in Leo's eyes. He fought back some sobs. His voice quivered a little as he said, "But I don't know what it is! Can you help me?" Then Nick said, "I'll see what I can do."

Leo stepped back from the old wooden counter and put his hands on his hips. "Well," he said, " I guess it is about time for me to go," and he took several steps toward the toyshop door. Then he paused, turned, and glanced around at all the toys on the shelves. "What are you going to do with all these toys?" he asked. Nick smiled and said, "They will find their way to where they are needed most."

The two hours Leo's daddy had given them to shop were almost gone. Leo hurried down Regalo Street back to Geschenk Street and southward toward where their car was parked. His sisters were already there, their arms cradling packages. Leo's daddy and mommy soon arrived, and they all got into the car for the ride back home. The sisters chattered so much Leo wondered if they had

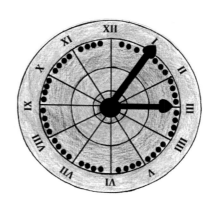

time to inhale a breath. He really did not listen to what they were talking about. He just sat in his seat quietly and looked out the car window at the snow that was starting to fall. When they got home everyone grabbed their packages and ran into the house. Nobody seemed to notice that Leo had nothing to carry in.

During that week, Leo's family put up their Christmas tree and placed colorful decorations all around their house. His sisters put their wrapped presents under the tree and sang carols. All the while, Leo would look at the gifts and feel bad that he had not found that special gift for his school friend. He thought and thought about what he could get his friend. But every time he came up with an idea, it just did not seem to be right. All he could think of were the toys in Nick's toyshop. In particular, Leo thought about the marbles. He knew his friend liked marbles, and if he had some they could play games together. But marbles were an expense his friend's family couldn't afford. And Leo didn't have marbles, either, so he could not give his friend any.

Christmas Eve arrived, and Leo kept thinking about the things in Nick's toyshop. Leo was determined to go back there and get something for his friend. He knew deep inside that such a gift would only be possible from Nick's toyshop. And he thought he could certainly explain to Nick why he needed a toy so much and could convince Nick to sell one to him. Nick just seemed like the kind of person who would listen and help out. So Leo talked his daddy into making another trip into town. Once there, Leo's daddy had to make a quick stop in the hardware store, and Leo walked north until he came to the pole that marked where Geschenk Street met Regalo Street. He quickly made his way to the old building where Nick's toyshop was located.

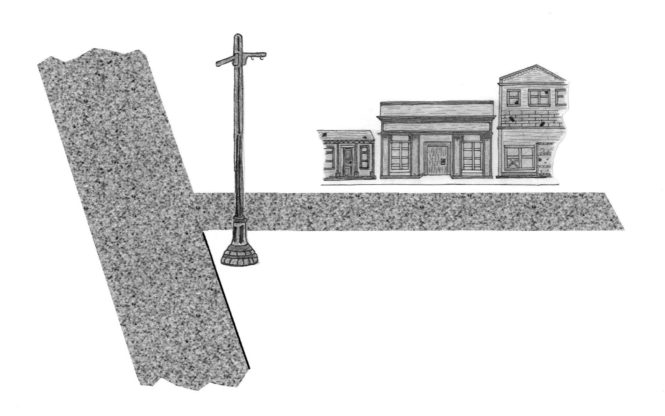

When Leo arrived at Nick's shop, he looked into the window. It was dark inside. Leo thought that was odd on Christmas Eve since most stores would be open to sell things to late shoppers. He reached down and grasped the old iron doorknob and turned it. The doorknob squeaked and the door opened with a quiet groan. Leo stepped inside on the old wooden floor that creaked under his foot. Leo looked around the shop and his heart sank. All the shelves were empty. There was not a single toy left anywhere. Leo called out for Nick. Silence. Nick was gone. Leo turned and walked out of the toyshop with his head hanging. A tear welled up in his eye as he slowly ambled back to Greschenk Street. He sat quietly in the seat next to his daddy as they drove home. His heart felt heavy. It seemed to take an extra long time to get home that day.

The next morning was Christmas day. Leo was warm and cozy huddled beneath the quilts and blankets on his bed. He really didn't want to get out of bed today. He did not want to face the fact that he had not been able to get that special gift for his friend.

The smell of Christmas breakfast wafted up from the kitchen, and before long Leo could not resist getting out of bed and going downstairs. As usual, his sisters were keeping up a continuous chatter and banter. He sat at the kitchen table staring down at his plate and glass of milk. Once he glanced up and saw his mommy looking at him. She was smiling her quiet, gentle smile. It helped Leo feel better. As the family sat around their breakfast table, there was a knock at their front door. Leo's daddy looked up, pushed himself back from the table and went to the front door. It was not long before his daddy walked back into the kitchen and looked straight at Leo. "Leo," he said, "there is someone at the front door who wants to see you." Leo wondered who it could be. Surely, it must be Nick! He had come to help! So Leo jumped from his chair and rushed to the front door. It was not Nick who was there. It was his friend from school.

His friend's face was glowing. His smile was from ear to ear and the light from the house gleamed on his teeth. He leapt forward and gave Leo a huge, long hug. Then he stepped back, reached into his coat pocket, and pulled out a small leather bag. He said, "Leo, I have always loved these things and always wanted some, but I never ever ever could get them. I know they came from you, and I wanted to come and thank you for making this the best Christmas I could ever have!" Leo didn't know what to say, and then looked down into the open leather bag in his friend's hands. Inside Leo could clearly see marbles.

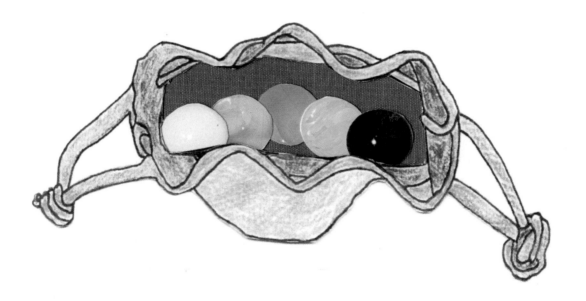

There was a white one, a green one, a yellow one, a blue one, and a black one. They were beautiful. They gleamed in the light and looked as precious as the most expensive and rarest jewels in the world. The white one was the purest white. The green one was forest green with lighter swirls of holly and grass green winding through it. The blue one had the deepest ocean blue ever seen. The yellow marble was a golden as the warming sun and ripe wheat, and the black one was a dark and pure as anthracite coal.

Leo was dumbfounded. "But I . . . I . . . I tried but couldn't . . . ." His friend interrupted him. "Thank you for this gift! I wish I had something for you!" And Leo said, "Your gift to me is our friendship!" Then the friend turned and walked off their porch to an old car in the street whose engine was running. His friend got in the car and it drove down the street sputtering and puffing out gray blue smoke. The falling snow soon made the old car disappear as it made its way to the end of the street.

Leo smiled and went back to the kitchen. "Who was it, dear?" asked his mommy. "It was a dear friend of mine." Leo said. "He wanted to wish me a happy Christmas." "Well," his mommy said, "that was so nice of him!" Leo looked down at his breakfast, and his heart felt warm. He almost had a tear of joy begin to form in his eye. Everything seemed unusually quiet at that moment, although the kitchen was anything but quiet with the clattering of dishes and his sisters' chattering. Then there was another knock at the front door. Leo thought it might be his friend coming back to spend some time enjoying playing with the wonderful marbles. He jumped from his chair and rushed to the door. He had the biggest smile when he threw open the door. As it swung wide, there was nobody there. He looked down the street first one way and then the other to see if that old car was anywhere in sight. The street was empty except for snow that was piling up on it from the snowfall. His smile melted away, and he turned to begin closing the door. As he turned, just before latching the door closed, he looked down and saw a small package on the door threshold.

The package could fit into his hand. He picked it up and looked at it. There was a small tag on it. The tag said, "For a dear friend." Leo closed the door and stepped backward toward the Christmas tree. There he sat down and slowly unwrapped the package. He removed the lid and with a surprise gasped as he looked into the box. There, down in the bottom of the box was a marble. It was a red one. In fact, it was crimson red. Leo lifted it out of the box and looked closely at it. As he turned it in his hand, he noticed the crimson color was pure throughout the entire marble – except for a tiny white spot just under the surface – a spot that looked just like a snowflake.

About the Author

Kevin Finson is a retired professor of science education. He taught 34 years at the college level, two at the high school level, and five at the middle school level. He is an earth scientist by training, but also has taught physical, life, and other sciences (as well as teaching on instructional theory and program evaluation). He is a vocal proponent of inquiry learning and teaching. Kevin has a sense of humor and really likes puns and shaggy dog stories. When at the university, he hosted an annual holiday party featuring a shaggy dog story contest. Since his retirement, he started to write children's books for his grandchildren. During his working career, Kevin was heavily involved in service to professional science education associations and maintained a consistent publication record that included the publication of eight books, some chapters and monographs, and a host of refereed (peer-reviewed) journal articles. Most of his professional academic publication focus has been on science for students with disabilities and on students' perceptions about scientists and visual data.

Other Children's Books by Kevin D. Finson that you and your children will enjoy:

This book is written for children ages 5 through 12. It is the story of how a thunderstorm forms and then passes. It is written in a rhyming narrative and includes original photographs of clouds.

This book is written for children ages 3 through 8 and presents the color spectrum nature reveals through flower blossoms. It is written in a rhyming narrative and includes original photographs of flower blossoms.

Christmas was coming, and Annie had no idea what to get for her mother as a present. What could she possibly get her mother that would show her how much she loved her? She had to make a decision sometime in the twelve days that were left before Christmas arrived. Come and journey with Annie each of those days as she searches for that perfect present. Then, discover what that very best gift actually was!

What was Starduster's purpose and role in God's plan to fill the universe with light and warmth? Come and share in Starduster's story as the very first star created by God in His plan to pierce the cold darkness of space and bring life into it. See how Starduster gave of itself in God's plan to make billions of stars and planets, and more specifically how it led to the creation of the earth and life on it. Find out how Starduster's legacy lives on in the guiding light illuminated by the Bethlehem Star. This story was inspired by a letter Kevin wrote to his granddaughter.

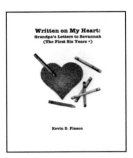

Travel along the road of life with Kevin and his granddaughters. He has undertaken the loving task of sharing with them episodic memories of his and their lives mixed with touches of science and history. From the day his grandchildren were born Kevin decided to write letters to Gabriella, Ivy, and Savannah each month, most of them on the day of the month on which each was born. This book is a compilation of the first ten years' worth of letters Kevin wrote to Gabriella, the first eight years to Ivy, and the first six to Savannah. It is through such letters that one can come closer to family and become more understanding of one's roots. These letters are more than just a diary since Kevin wrote them to his grandchildren rather than to himself. The purpose of each letter is to provide short stories in the context of real life and how it relates to growth and development in one's faith in God. The central message is to seek ways to have a strong faith and unwavering trust in God as she navigates the roads of life that lie before her.

Made in the USA
Las Vegas, NV
01 November 2022

58534169R00024